Angel in the Tower

Written and Illustrated by
ELIZABETH DRALLE

FARRAR STRAUS & CUDAHY
New York

Bell Books

Angel in
The Tower

To My Mother

*who always thought any of
her children could do* anything;

*without the confidence she engendered
I should never have been so brash
as to think I could write a book.*

Angel in the Tower

1

Angel sat up and rubbed his eyes. He no sooner had the right one open than the left one would go to sleep again. But the bells were ringing, ringing loud! Miguel was ringing them all alone, and he would be finished before Angel was there to help him if Angel didn't hurry!

Angel rolled out of his covers and stumbled up the stairs. The stones felt cold to his bare feet, and he was glad of the warm sunshine at the top. Fastening the shoulder straps of his overalls, he ran to the ropes.

All around him the bells were ringing. "Bong . . . bong . . . bong . . ." boomed the big, big bell that weighed so many kilograms that Angel always gasped when Miguel told the tourists. Angel didn't know just how many, because he could only count to six, and after that things were "a great many."

The Lady Bell had a deep throaty tone, but a lady-like lilt at the end of each peal: "D . . . up! D . . . up!" Espíritu Santo was ringing, and all the other bells. Only Angelino was silent.

Miguel was laughing. Surrounded by ropes laced together so that he could sound all the bells with only two hands and two feet, he looked like a happy human spider in his web. "Ah!" he cried, as he pulled and stretched, and the heavy hammers swung to the sides of the two bells he was working with his right hand. "Bing! Dang!" rang the bells, and nearly drowned out his laughter as he shouted, "Oh, see him yawn! All the world will know that you didn't get up when Angelino does not ring this morning!"

Angel quickly unwound from its wooden peg the rope of the smallest bell, and heaved his small weight against that of the clapper. As the "Ding! . . . ding! . . . ding!" of Angelino piped into the general clamor, he raised his soft eyes and smiled in return.

He hadn't long to ring, for he had been very late. When Miguel tied up his ropes, Angel tied his quickly and ran to his father. "Your blessing, sir!" he asked with bowed head. Miguel bared his own dark head and blessed the little boy, then lifted him to his shoulder and started down the narrow circular stairs.

Angel wrapped his arm around his father's head, tipping his hat over his eye, while he tickled him under the chin. "Grrrrr!" growled Miguel. "I am a lion, and I'll chew those fingers off! GRRRRRR!"

Angel giggled delightedly. Today Miguel was a lion. Every morning the game was different. All the animals in the zoo came to town, one by one, and Angel rode on their backs, down, down, down, the stairs, and home to the landing.

Before the door was opened, they could smell the warm, sweet, delicious, breakfast tortillas, and today, chocolate too!

Angel slid down the lion's back and stood before his mother. María smiled at him gently and blessed his tousled head. "Now Angel, comb your hair, and wash your face and neck, and don't forget your ears!"

"Every morning I hear that," he thought. "Wouldn't you think that my own mother would see how grown-up I am? But always, 'Angel, wash your neck!'" Out loud he said, "Yes, my mother!"

"We will need water. I have used the last."

"Yes, my mother."

"You will get us some?"

"Yes, my mother!"—this time with a note of pride, as he swung the towel across the back of his neck and dived for the water can that was his glory, the symbol of his pride in his family and the evidence that he was growing up, and could, every day, contribute to the work of the world by bringing up the water.

Joyfully he swung the gasoline can with a wooden bar stretched between the sides, a fine big pail for so small a boy, and padded down the stairs. Sometimes the can hit the stone wall and made an echoing sound, but except for that, all was quiet here within the four sides of the dim cool tower.

Around and around and around, and down, down, down he went, out into the brilliant sunshine, across the courtyard, through the tall bronze fence, across the sidewalk beside the flower vendor and the seller of rosaries. Across the street and through the garden of the plaza and up to the fountain they went—Angel and the gasoline-can pail.

"A big boy can carry a pail *full!*" said Angel; so he filled it.

He lifted it over the broad edge and set it onto the ground. That was odd! It was heavy, just as heavy as it had been the day before—and yet he was older today!

"It does not matter," said Angel. "Maybe I am just not *that* big yet . . . a big boy but not a very big boy!"

He dumped a little water on the flowers in the beds by the tile walk and started off again.

But as he stepped from the light gold sunshine around the fountain through the cool purple shadows of the almond trees, the pail seemed to get heavier and heavier. Angel sat on one of the stone benches by the sidewalk and swung his legs while he thought about things. He could look up from his seat and see the bells, so high up that they looked small. There they hung in the tower of the cathedral, their deep bronze glow so beautiful against the deep blue sky that Angel sighed and smiled happily to think that he lived so close to them. "Like the angels," his mother always said. "Like the angels," he echoed in his thoughts.

Angel slid from the seat and picked up the water can again. He felt very happy and sloshed a little water onto his toes so that they could wiggle around in it and be happy too. Then he set the pail on the bench and ran back to the fountain where he dipped his hands into the water and threw it over his face and neck.

His wet face shone like the bells he loved so well as he skipped back to his water pail. As he picked it up, he stared at the mosaic inlay in the back of the bench. He must ask about that again, he decided. It was a beautiful story, but he forgot it a little.

Slowly and carefully he lifted the pail to his shoulder as he had seen his father do, and was surprised to find that it wasn't so heavy as he had thought.

Balancing it carefully on his shoulder and upturned

palm, and with his other hand on the edge, he walked across the sidewalk, skirting a man carrying a load of chairs and a blind old Indian man begging near the curb. Across the street he went, turning his whole body to watch out for traffic, since he couldn't see past the tall can.

"Buenas días!" to the flower vendor and "Buenas días!" to the seller of rosaries and holy cards, and then up the short stone steps and through the door into the cool green shadows of the tower, then up and up and up until Angel was quite out of breath. He set the pail down and rested, sitting on the warm step with his foot against the pail's cool side.

He tried a few experimental "Booms" and listened to the echo resound, "BOOM, Boom, boom" up the tower.

His mother tried an experimental call "Angel," and again the sound repeated, "ANGEL, Angel, angel" down the tower.

"Yes, Mama—a little moment," he answered, and "A LITTLE MOMENT, Moment, moment," said the echo.

Again the pail was lifted, and the slow ascent begun —step after step after step, and the boy grew wearier with each of them, but at last he stood on the platform near his home and took the few last steps up to his own door.

"You were a long time, baby!" His mother smiled at him.

"You should not call me 'baby,' " he reproached her. "Only a big boy could carry such a big pail of water."

"Such a big pail, true—but only half full." She laughed.

Angel looked, and indeed his mother was not teasing him, for it was no more than half full.

"But I do not understand," he protested, wide-eyed. "I filled it very full at the fountain!"

"It does not matter. It is enough."

But to Angel it did matter. It mattered very much, and as he ate his breakfast he wondered about it . . . about how much work it was to carry up so little water . . . about where the water went to, when he remembered filling the can to the brim . . . about many things that he did not understand.

"Mother," he asked, "will you tell me again the story of the picture on the bench?"

"Yes, my darling, later."

"Who is on the bench?" asked his father.

"It is the city seal, Miguel. The boy likes the story of the picture."

"Oh, yes, of course—and do you know it?" he asked, turning to Angel.

"Only a little, Father."

"But that is good, very good, that you should know these things," his father said, rising and patting Angel on the head.

"A fine boy we have," he said, as he reached for his hat.

"A fine *big* boy," said Angel's mother. "Do not forget *that*. He is a big help to me. I don't know what I'd do without him."

Angel shyly looked down at his foot and felt very proud and happy that he was a help.

2

Every day, as soon as breakfast was finished, Angel and his mother went to the market, for there was no way of keeping food fresh from one day to another— no refrigerator nor icebox.

Each day they would take a basket and a bag and go down and down and down to the street, and then across the pavement and through the high fence and past the flower vendor and the sleeping seller of rosaries, and across the sidewalk and the street and down the street under the arcade with shops that sold candy and carved marble and onyx, and shops that sold carved wood, and the candle shop and a restaurant, then across the street and down the narrow sidewalk for a block and a half and through the round arch and —*the market.*

Oh, the lovely babel of all the vendors vying for customers and the children running in and out carrying packages for lady shoppers! The color of the draped clothes: shirts, overalls, shawls and uncut cloth and embroideries! The flower market and the vegetable market! The breads and cakes and fruits! And the toys and dishes and pots and stoves! It was a won-

derful place, the like of which one cannot describe.

Some of the shops and stalls were indoors and some outdoors, and some sold spices and herbs and teas. The cooking that was going on! Such savory odors of all kinds that Angel couldn't just sniff; he had to inhale as deeply as he could, and when he thought he'd burst he exhaled suddenly and tried again. It was too much to try to smell the carnations and the fried pork and the chocolate and cinnamon and the vanilla and the roses all at once. So the last time he passed each he gave an extra sniff so that he could save it up until the next day when he would come again.

Always he padded after his mother to the vegetable section and saw the little green peppers in small piles and near them the green beans and the tomatoes, the potatoes and the okra, each in a little pile as high as his hand was wide. As his mother bargained and slowly added things to the basket, Angel carried her purchases and gazed down one aisle or another at the lovely things and the people.

There were mothers with babies on their backs and young girls with ribbons in their hair and charros with their tight-fitting trousers with braid and ornaments, and horses and donkeys, and ladies shopping with their little housemaids carrying their baskets—and many more. It was wonderful!

Once Angel had even seen a torero! But he didn't

have his cape on, and Angel would not have known
he was a real bullfighter if the other boys had not told
him. He was eating a pineapple.

Every day was wonderful in the market, but
Wednesday was the best. On Wednesday the people
from miles around came hurrying down the hillsides
carrying all kinds of things to the market—blankets
and serapes, belts with birds and people and animals
all woven into the red and black and white threads,
leather belts, pottery of all sizes and shapes, and vegetables and fruit. Each man and woman and even each
boy and girl had a load strapped to his back—a very
large one for the father, not quite such a big one for
the mother, and smaller ones for the children.

Angel could see them from the tower when they
were still a long way off. They looked very small on
the hills.

"Look!" he once shouted. "They look like ants
coming down the hillside."

"And they work like ants," said Miguel. "See how
much they carry!"

"They must be very tired," said Angel. "Why
don't they set their loads down and rest? Look, Father, they are all running!"

And it was true! They didn't run fast, but they
trotted right along mile after mile, without stopping.
Miguel and Angel watched them for a while. Then

Angel asked, "Why are they running, Father?"

Miguel pursed his mouth solemnly. "It is so that they will get to the market before they get tired," he said.

Angel thought. Then he shouted, "You're only teasing me again! How would that help? They'd only get tired all the faster!" He scowled furiously.

Miguel laughed loudly and patted him on the back. "You are growing up, little son. You are learning to think for yourself, I see. That is good! Very good! Soon I won't be able to tease you any more. You will know too much."

"Then tell me, Father, why do they run?" he persisted.

As they watched the tiny specks that were people gradually come nearer to the city, they could see which were men and women and which children, and Miguel explained:

"When a person has so much weight on his back, it is pushing him ahead like this"—and he pushed Angel gently between the shoulder blades. "When he has a great, great weight he has to either keep going ahead, or bend over toward the ground, to keep his load from knocking him down, and to keep his load in balance. You try it some time, but don't use a load of pottery; you may not be so good at it as those people."

Angel was better satisfied, but he always thought

about that when he saw the people with the big loads, and wondered whether any of them ever stubbed his toe.

Angel's mother always went to the market early, very early, so that all the food would be fresh and she would have first choice. Each thing was picked out carefully, for when you haven't very much money you must be very careful with what you have.

Slowly the basket would be filled, and Angel would trot after his mother who had the eggs in her bag. Sometimes, as today, they would buy some flowers— calla lilies or carnations, or daisies. No gardenias—they were only for dead people.

They priced the flowers at first one stand and then another, and at last bought a huge bouquet of red carnations. The flower-seller said one peso, but Angel's mother knew how to bargain, so she bought them for fifty centavos. The flower man wrapped the stems with raffia and made a loop in it for carrying the flowers. Angel slipped it over his right wrist and carried the basket in his left hand.

"Look," he called to his mother, "I look like a donkey—a pack on each side!"

"But such a nice little donkey," agreed María, stroking his shoulder. "Giddap, little donkey, and take our dinner to our house." María pulled her shawl

tight around her shoulders and back they went, through the arch and up the narrow street that by now had sunshine on one sidewalk. They went across the street and under the arcade where there were now scallops of sunshine on the colored tile, past the restaurants and the shops, across the street and up the steps.

The rosary-seller called a greeting, and María answered for them both.

"You must excuse my little donkey. He can only say, 'Hee haw,' but he works very well!"

The seller of rosaries laughed. "Ah, what a fine little donkey! How much do you want for him?"

Angel giggled and María explained, "Oh, he is not for sale. I only just bought him at the market. He was very expensive! The best they had!"

"Then I guess I cannot have one. I am very poor—" began the rosary-seller.

"Then it is a good thing your wares don't weigh much," said María, and they both laughed. María tucked a carnation into the old woman's hair. "From Our Lady of Guadalupe," she explained.

"Is that who you think *you* are?" The old lady was shocked. "The saints preserve us! And may God forgive you! Now in my day—"

"Oh no, no, no!" said María, making the sign of the

cross. "No, no, no! It is that we have bought them for the altar, but Our Lady will not mind that I give one to you who are named for her!"

"Oh, may she pray for us! Thank you, thank you,"

mumbled old Lupe. "And bless your fine donkey!" she said, recovering her spirits.

María and Angel said good-by hastily and were on the stairs to their own house before they laughed.

"Why did she scold you, Mother?" he asked.

"It is all right," said María. "Lupe is a good, kind woman. She did not understand what I meant." But she laughed too, as they climbed up, and up, and up, to their home.

3

All over the roof of the cathedral were tiles of beautiful colors, yellow and blue and white, shining in the morning sunlight. Each was only about as large as Angel's hand, but they were set next to each other carefully and neatly until they covered all the dome and curves, except for the big stone ribs that supported the whole church roof. Up and down the ribs were steps cut so that the workmen could climb all over the roof easily and safely without stepping on the beautiful but slippery tiles.

From down in the street one could not see the steps, nor could one see that there was a design painted onto each tile in the whole roof.

"There are thousands of them," said Miguel. "More than *six*," echoed Angel.

Neither could anyone see that down in the valley between the six arches of the roof Angel's mother spread her laundry on the clean tiles to dry.

From the windows in his house, Angel could see the lovely roof, and, on one spot, the sundial like a "U" of stone against the yellow and blue of tile. The shadow was falling from the right side to the six on the left side. He would ring his bell presently, and later he would have to ring it again when the shadow from the left side fell onto the six on the right side. But that was a long time off, and, except for bringing the water and carrying the food from the market, he had the day free, to think about his problem—a big problem which troubled him more and more each day.

Today he would talk to his father about it. As they rang the bells, Angel pulling the rope of the smallest and Miguel pulling all the rest, the big man watched the boy thoughtfully. He had talked very little this morning and María had said that he'd been very quiet yesterday too. Miguel hoped his small son was not ill.

The ringing was ended and the ropes were tied, and Angel had received his breakfast and was eating it slowly before he mentioned what was on his mind.

"Father—" he said, and stopped.

"Yes, my son," Miguel encouraged.

"Father, I shall soon be a man."

Miguel did not smile. "Yes, soon, but not *very* soon."

"No, but soon, and I shall do a man's work!" persisted the boy.

"Yes, of course!"

"And, Father, I should learn how now, so I can work well then."

There, it was out. Angel felt a little frightened at having said it, that he wanted to go out and work. He waited for his answer.

"Yes, my son, but there is time enough for that!"

"But things are very expensive," Angel urged. "Each day at the market—so *much* money! If I could only earn a little!" His small face gazed up at Miguel earnestly as the big man nodded.

"Yes, my boy—but we must think it over. Your mother and I will talk of this."

"But you said yesterday that I was growing up and learning to think for myself. Is it not right that I should work for myself too? You should not feed me forever!"

Miguel sighed and patted the boy's shoulder. "A fine boy! We shall see! We shall see!"

That day Angel wandered to the market and decided that if he had to wait until his parents had talked it over, there was still no harm in looking around to see what kind of job he'd like best. As he walked he de-

cided he would not like to sell rosaries nor flowers; he'd rather keep them, they were so pretty. He didn't want to work in a shop of any kind, nor in a restaurant.

A bus came around the corner, and, as it swerved by, Angel thought maybe he'd like to drive a bus, but was afraid he wasn't quite big enough. Now an airplane—maybe he could drive that. It couldn't be so heavy as a bus because airplanes were so light they floated in the air. Angel wondered where a small boy learned to drive an airplane. He wondered where the airplanes stopped and was afraid it must be a long distance away and that maybe he couldn't get home for supper—maybe not even in time to ring the bell! But if he were going to drive an airplane, he'd better start soon. It might take a long, long time to learn how.

Angel sauntered down the narrow street wondering which was better, airplanes or bells.

Crash! The noise was so loud that for a moment Angel couldn't decide whether it was an airplane or a bell that had fallen. Other people on the street started to run toward the arched entrance to the market, and Angel found himself with them surging toward the loud noise.

People's legs were in his way, but by wiggling a little and crawling a little he got to the front row.

Then he saw the bus and the loud noise, or at least

he saw what had made it. A donkey cart had been hit by the bus. It was turned over, and crates of chickens had been hurled all over the road. One crate had opened and out flew all the chickens! The chickens cackled! The donkey bawled! The man shouted! The bus driver bellowed! And everybody told everyone else what had happened.

"It was the bus driver," cried one man.

"No, no, you are mistaken," said another man. "In truth, it was the donkey driver! He should not have backed through the archway."

"But I did not back through the archway!" shouted the driver. "It was the donkey! I drove him forward into the market, but because he is a donkey, when I drove him forward he backed into the street. And see my chickens! All my chickens! All over the street!"

The chickens squawked and flew around the circle made by the crowd, but all the people were so busy arguing that they ignored them.

Angel caught a chicken and put it into the coop. Then another, and another—and at last they were all safe again, but still the argument continued. The chickens cackled. The donkey bawled.

"It was not my fault," the donkey's owner shouted. "If you did not drive so fast you could have stopped. My donkey had no right to back up, but you should have stopped!"

The crowd sided with the chicken man. "Yes, it is true," they said, nodding their heads.

"But I did you no harm!" The bus driver tried to defend himself.

"No harm indeed! Look at my beautiful cart! Look at my chicken crate! Look at my chickens! Look at my donkey—hear how unhappy he is!"

"What is the matter with your cart?" asked the bus driver.

It was true that the cart, which by now was upright again, showed little damage. It was rough, unpainted and balanced on two wheels—and if it had a few new scratches they didn't show on its aged wood. The chicken crate had been a homemade one, and now that the cover was back in place it seemed as good as it ever had been.

"It is ruined!" wailed the chicken man. "What will my wife say?"

The crowd nodded heads in agreement. What would the man tell his wife?

"It is not damaged," declared the bus driver.

"But can you convince my wife of that? She is an obstinate woman!"

"Look, your chickens are all right too. They're all back in their coop!"

"Oh no—they are worthless! Look, I will give them away." And so saying, the man threw open the cover

of the crate, gathered one big chicken, and thrust it into Angel's arms.

"—all of them—" he continued distractedly, and another was squawking in Angel's surprised grasp.

"Stop! Stop!" cried the bus driver. "What are you doing? How much is the damage I have done worth?"

The chicken man looked dubious.

"Well?" said the harried bus driver, thrusting his hand into the pocket of his faded uniform.

"Look!" said the chicken man. "Will you give me a ride on your bus?"

"Yes," said the driver, "any time you like."

"And every time?"

"Yes, every time."

The chicken man's face beamed. He turned and spoke to the crowd, turning a full circle: "You heard him. He said he would give me a ride every time I wanted."

"But only on *my* bus," hastily added the bus driver.

"Every day?"

"If you like."

"No, I cannot go every day. I am a man of business," he added gruffly, making his face solemn as he addressed the bus driver, "with more to do than ride on buses every day. I shall ride only four days a week."

He turned back to the crowd, grinning happily.

"You have heard him say that I may ride in his bus *free?*"

A chorus of "Yes" answered him.

"All right," said the defeated bus driver, "I'll see you later."

"Yes, later," agreed the crowd, waving good-by to him, then pressing around the chicken man to congratulate him. "Just think!" "How fortunate!" "What a lucky man!"

Angel elbowed his way to the man. "Here are your chickens, sir!"

At first no one heard him through the chorus of congratulations. He had to speak again and again. Finally the fortunate man noticed him. "Oh, yes! Keep them, my boy—and welcome," he said with a big gesture. "Such a small price to pay to ride on the bus as often as I please!"

Angel gasped at such beneficence and hugged the fowls till they squawked. He quickly wiggled his way back through the crowd, a chicken under each arm. He ran all the way home! He puffed and panted up all the steps of the tower with his wonderful present!

He couldn't open the door with both arms full of the chickens and couldn't call because there wasn't any breath left in his body, but he bumped the door a little and María heard him and opened it and her mouth both at once.

"Where did you get the chickens?" she cried, but before he could have answered—if he had been able to—she called, "Miguel! Miguel! Come and see Angel's chickens!"

Miguel came hurrying down from the bell platform. "Where did the chickens come from?" he cried.

"The chicken man gave them to me because the bus man gave him a ride in the bus every day."

"And he could not take the chickens on the bus? But why he didn't sell them?"

"Because the bus man ran into his cart."

"Couldn't the cart be fixed?"

"Oh, the cart wasn't hurt!"

María stood laughing at the two of them and at the chickens running around the room.

"You had better start at the beginning and take your time, son. What happened first?"

Angel took a deep breath and tried again. He told about the bus and the cart and the donkey and the cart driver. He told about the argument and at last about the chickens. When he had finished, his father and mother were both holding their sides.

"A fine dinner we will have," said Miguel.

"Oh, Father, do we have to cook them? Do we have to kill them?"

"And what else?"

"Couldn't I keep them? I'll take care of them myself. I'll feed them."

"But where would you keep chickens? You and your mother and I do not have too much room in our home that we should share it with chickens!"

"But I could keep them on the roof! Please, Father."

"On the roof! On the roof of a cathedral?"

"But, Father, no one would know. See, the tiles are slippery, so the chickens couldn't walk up, and I can put a board on the steps so they can't go up there either. No one will know!"

"But where would your mother put her wash?"

"I will carry it to the other side of the dome. Please, Father, and we can eat all the eggs instead of the chickens. Or we can save the eggs and have lots more chickens. Maybe we could even sell them—"

"Enough! Enough!" His father threw up his hands. "With such a businessman in the house we'll soon be millionaires! But what will his excellency, the Archbishop, say?"

"He will not know. He is too old to climb up here, and anyway, he would not care so long as they did not give scandal," pleaded María.

"Oh, my little wife is lonely for the farm from which I took her to my heaven in the sky! If you want them, they shall stay! I suppose I should be glad you don't want a cow," laughed Miguel. "What are their names?"

They all sat down and thought about it.

Angel wanted to call them "Juárez" and "Venestiana Cerranza," after two national heroes, but Miguel said no. They were only chickens and should not bring ridicule on great names. María suggested "Petro" and "Paulo," but Miguel said that those names would be still worse, and not only disrespectful but blasphemous.

Miguel said, "Why don't you call them 'bus driver' and 'chicken cart man,' if you have to call them after men?"

Angel didn't think those names were very good. Miguel said, "Anyway, you can name only one a man's name, because the other is a lady chicken."

So they thought some more.

Finally Angel brightened. "I will call them 'Horse' and 'Cow,' " he said. "The lady chicken can be 'Cow' and the man 'Horse.' Then we will have a whole farm on the roof and Mother will not be lonely any more!"

Miguel and María laughed so hard that they cried. "Who would have thought of such fine names except our son?" they said.

4

Angel had helped ring the bells and then he had run all the way down to the market twice: once for the groceries and once for something María had forgotten the first time. María had said that she was very sorry to ask him to go again, that maybe she should go after it herself, but Angel said that he would be very glad to go. But after he started up the stairs again, he felt very tired and had to rest three times on the way up.

"Some time," he thought, "I'll be a big man and I'll be able to go up those steps faster and easier." Sitting on the broad cool step, puffing, he gazed out of the slit in the thick stone wall of the tower and looked a long way off in the distance and wondered what kind of people lived on the other side of the mountains, and what kind of people lived beyond them, and what kind of houses they lived in.

"Well," he said, "When I'm big enough, so that I don't get tired, I'll walk all the way over there some morning and be back again before dinner. I'll carry some tortillas with me so I won't get hungry."

"Angel!" He heard his mother's voice. "Angelino!"

Reluctantly he withdrew his gaze from the hills, picked up his package, and trudged up the steps.

María pushed the hair off his damp forehead and kissed him. "I am sorry to make you so tired, my little one."

Angel drew himself up proudly. "It was a pleasure, Mother! I am not at all tired. But this is a very good material. The woman in the market said so."

Watching his mother unfold the cloth, his eyes glowed. It had cost a whole peso and his mother had let him carry the money in his own hand.

"Is it the right thing, my mother?"

"Yes, my son, it is quite perfect."

It would not have been polite to ask what his mother would do with the cloth. He waited for her to say, but she stroked his hair and turned again to patting the thin pancakes, so Angel picked up a dish of crumbs and went out to feed the chickens.

Absent-mindedly he scattered them and watched the rooster pecking, pecking.

"Horse is very hungry today," he called to his mother. He watched a little longer, then picked up the water dish and carried it into the house and washed it. He filled it with clear water and carried it to the chickens.

But still there was only the rooster.

"Cow! Cow!" he called, searching for the hen. Where could she be? The roof was too slippery for her to climb. Could she have fallen off? There was no dog nor cat to hurt her.

"Cow! Cow!"

"Cackle! Cackle!"

Where had it come from? He tried again.

"Cow! Cow!"

"Cackle! Cackle!"

Suddenly he looked up. There she sat under one horn of the sun dial! She must have flown up and couldn't get down. Angel was very much distressed.

"Oh, you poor little hen! My poor little cow! Poor little bird! Don't be afraid. I am coming, little Cow!"

"Cackle! Cackle!"

At last he reached her and gathered the fat bird in his arms, and then he saw it—an egg! Angel was so excited he didn't know what to do.

"Mama! Mama!" he shrieked.

María hurried to the door wiping her hands. "What is it, my Angel? What is it?"

"An egg, my mother! Cow has laid an egg!"

"Oh a great marvel! A great good fortune!"

"But what shall I do?"

"Just bring her some water and some food and she will take care of it for you. Soon you will see a baby chicken from the egg."

"Truly?"

"Truly, my son!"

Angel hurried around making the hen comfortable. He brought her food and water. An old piece of cloth made a nest for the bird. An old piece of sacking made a shelter in case it might rain, or the sun be too strong.

Angel stood twisting his finger around and around in the button hole of his overall straps. What else could he do to make his hen comfortable? He watched her for a while, but she seemed content, so he mopped up the little "chicken yard" and went into the house.

"Will you tell me again about the angels, Mother?" he asked as he poked more charcoal into the little fire-box of the stove.

The light shown on her face and on her black hair. Angel thought, "I have the most beautiful mother in the world!"

"What did you say, my son?"

"Tonight, tonight maybe, you will tell me again the story of the angels?"

"Of course, dear. I shall tell you now. We will have time before your father comes for his supper."

Angel brought more wood so that it would be convenient when needed and settled himself comfortably. He knelt beside his mother on the mat and rested against her. She put her arm around him, but didn't cease in her pat, pat, patting of the tortillas.

"It was many many years ago," she began. "There was no city here then, no market, no churches, no stores and very few houses. Not big houses—just a few small houses—but there were very good people living in them. They were so good and so hard-working that

they wanted to build to God a very great church, a cathedral.

"They made great plans and all worked very hard to build the church. All day long they labored, from early dawn until dark, and at dawn the next day they started again, and the next day and the next the same way. They worked happily and did not quarrel nor speak cross words. Only good things came from their lips and only good deeds came from their hands. And the church went up so fast! The great blocks of stone were not so heavy as they had seemed, and when the men came in the morning there was more of the building completed than they had remembered from the night before. Each day this happened, and when their wives brought them their dinner at noon, they were always surprised at the industry that had accomplished so much.

"Then the story started. It was said that at night, while the men slept, angels came and carried on the work. It was said that some angels carried stones, and others mortar, and others laid them in place. But when the men returned each morning, the angels had left and did not return until darkness had stopped the labor of the men. And so it was that night and day the work never stopped, but was carried on for the glory of God."

"And that is why the picture is on the park bench!" interrupted her audience.

"Yes," said his mother, smiling, "that is the seal of the city. It is a picture of the cathedral with the angels flying above it, and one angel has a stone and the other a trowel of mortar. They are building the cathedral. That is why the city is called Puebla of the Angels."

"But is it true, Mama?"

"Who knows? But it is believed to be true."

"But you said it was true about the egg!"

"Yes, my son. That I have seen with my own eyes. The angels I did not see. It was before my lifetime. But if the egg is true it is not less miraculous, so this story may well be true also. Who knows?"

5

All day long Angel was busy. There were the pails of water and the vegetables and the bells—so many errands. Up and up and up and up, and puff and puff and pant, and a look at the chickens—and then down again.

Sometimes, as he darted across streets and along sidewalks, he saw other boys on their way to or from school. Their books were in little boxes fastened to straps through which they slipped their arms, so that the box would rest on their shoulders and leave their hands free. Once he heard two boys talking about school and stood near by and listened. He knew that he should not do this, but he had asked his mother and father about this thing called "school" and they had said that they did not know. They had never been there.

Today the boys were talking about something in a book. They were pointing their fingers at a spot near the middle of a page.

One said, "But it says here that . . ."

Angel listened, but he didn't hear the book say anything.

The other said, "No, it says . . ." And Angel thought that maybe the book didn't speak very loudly. He stepped a little closer, the better to hear what the book was saying.

One of the boys noticed him and said, "Look, we

will ask this boy which is right! Read what the book says right here and tell us what you think it means."

Angel peered at the spot on which the boy's finger rested. "I am sorry," he said. "Please excuse me, but I hear nothing."

"But you did not read it. Read it aloud and tell us what it means."

Angel looked at the marks on the page.

"Read?" he asked. "This I do not know. What is this 'read'?"

"But don't you read?" "Don't you read at all?"

"With your permission," he explained politely, "I do not. If it is to be regretted, I am sorry. Perhaps if you will tell me . . ."

The boys stopped their argument to explain what reading was. They felt very conscious of their superior knowledge and delighted to impart it to Angel.

Angel asked them if it were possible to write "egg." They said yes, and wrote the word on the sidewalk.

Angel was delighted and thanked them very much. After they left, he traced the letters again and again. On his return from the market, he set his basket down and gazed at the word again so that he would remember it and be able to draw it for his mother when he had climbed the steps.

This time he climbed all the stairs without stopping. He didn't dare rest for fear he might forget the magic

word. When he staggered into the room, his mother looked up from her work, smiling.

"Mama, Mama!" he cried. "I have a word!"

Angel seized a piece of the charcoal, and on the stone floor near the wall, where it was not covered by the grass mat, he drew the letters, the wonderful word —EGG.

"And what is it?" his mother asked.

"It is 'egg,'" he cried.

"But not a good egg. You cannot eat it. It will not hatch into a chicken!"

"But you do not understand, my mother! It is a word, a new thing, and it means 'egg.' There are things like this for all words. They are in a book. A boy showed it to me."

"A book? And were there pictures?"

"No, I did not see any, only things like this. But they had other books. There may be pictures in those."

"Who had the books?"

"The boys who go to school."

"To school! If that is all they have in that place it cannot be worth much!"

"But it is, my mother!"

"To me it seems a bad thing. We will talk of it with your father."

Nothing was said until Miguel's return. Angel fed the chickens in silence and silently changed the water in their dish. In silence he ate his supper alone, for his father was late in returning. It was not the silence of anger nor of fear, but the silence of not knowing what to say and so saying nothing.

Finally Miguel returned, and after he had eaten, his wife and son laid the matter before him.

"To me it seems bad," said María. "But to you, a man of the world, it may have some value."

Miguel drew himself up straight. "This thing, this word," he asked gravely, "it is 'egg'?"

"Yes, they have said so," answered the boy.

"But it is on the floor. Is it 'egg' if it is on the wall?"

"So I believe." Angel's head nodded vigorously.

"And is it 'egg' if it is in a book?"

"That also I believe."

"And if on a little slip of paper?"

"Yes, Father."

His father's face cleared. "So!" He turned to his wife. "So! It is not a thing of evil. I believe it to have value."

María looked relieved. "Yes?" She said eagerly. "It is not bad?"

"No, it is good," Miguel assured her. "It can be written on a paper. Therefore you may put it on a piece of paper and tie a stone to it and drop it from the window and Angel can pick it up from the ground and will know your need of eggs when he sees that on the paper."

"But would it not be easier to draw a picture of an egg? I could do it more easily. And there are no stones up here so far from the ground, and if I did drop a stone, it might hit someone on the head and kill him."

"Yes. You speak the truth. It cannot be done, but the word has possibilities."

"Then it will be all right for me to talk to the boys from the school? I may learn another word with your permission?"

"Yes, but not too much. You do no wrong, but it is better to spend men's time in something useful. This word 'egg' has possibilities, but no practical use."

6

After that Angel waited each day for the boys to come from school. He hurried so that he could not play "animals" with his father but ran down to the street as soon as the bells were rung. Each day the boys taught him a new word—"beans," "corn," "peppers," "salt." Each one was carefully memorized and written on the floor of his tower home, near to the wall where it wouldn't be lost when the floor was swept. Angel wasn't sure how it would be managed, but he was sure he'd need the words in his plan.

One day he decided to ask to be taught "water." He had been waiting for the boys for some time when finally they came and he saw why they were late. They were tossing something into the air and watching it float down.

"What is it?" he called.

"Only a handkerchief," the bigger boy explained. "See, we have a string tied to each corner. Then all the strings are tied together to a stone. I wrap the stone in the handkerchief and throw it into the air. So!"

Angel watched the folds of cloth snap into a neat little umbrella and float gently to the earth.

"Is it permitted that I try it?" he asked.

"Of course!" they agreed and watched Angel throw it again and again.

They had forgotten the word that Angel was to learn that day, and he didn't like to remind them. However, when they had hurried home he had his plan made. He carried a stone upstairs with him.

That night he begged from his mother a piece of cloth from his old overalls. He tore it into a square. His mother's thread made the cords and the stone was tied to the threads.

Angel tossed it into the air. His mother watched him silently until then. However, this was too much.

"Angelino!" she cried. "First you tear up a piece of cloth that could well be used to make patches, or for cleaning or for polishing. Then you use my thread as if it did not cost money to buy—and now throwing stones, and in the house! It is too much! Is it such things you learn when you talk to the boys from the school?"

"But it worked very well for them, Mother!"

"What worked—the overalls? Or the stone? They are industrious overalls that work with no one in them!"

"It made a little umbrella that floated down slowly."

"Let me see it—but let it float on the roof, not in the house."

But no matter how much he tried, Angel couldn't make it work.

Finally he tied his handkerchief in place of the overall patch. He made the strings shorter, then longer. At last it performed.

"Mother, Mother mine!" he called, and María came out to see it.

"Watch, if you please," he shouted and then threw it into the air. It floated down slowly. Angel retrieved it and threw it again. It floated down gently. "Don't you see what it will do?" he cried as he threw it.

"Yes, it is very amusing," his mother conceded.

"But it is useful!" he answered. "You would not toss the stone down from the window with the note attached; you were afraid the stone might hurt someone. But not this little umbrella. You can throw the note with the words written on it from the tower, and I can pick it up from the pavement."

"What? You expect that I, your mother, should throw toys off roofs? What would the Archbishop say? What would he think of the dignity of the bell-ringers if they should take to throwing umbrellas out of the tower? Please, my son! Remember that you were named from the name of the cathedral, that your father was named for St. Miguel the Archangel, that he and his father before him were bell-ringers in this glorious cathedral! Do not disgrace them."

Angel stood with bowed head and flushed face.

"Excuse it, please! I meant no disrespect to the cathedral nor to you, my mother."

His penitence was so abject that his mother's face softened in spite of herself. She gazed at his bowed head.

"Yes, I know that. You are a good boy, but you must think of those things, of the dignity of your mother and of your father's work."

Angel felt baffled. It had seemed such a good idea, but he could now see that it had disadvantages. Reluctantly he tucked the toy into his pocket. He must think of another plan. Suddenly his face brightened and he went to look at the egg and then up to the tower to ring his bell.

7

Nearly every day the words along the edge of the floor gained by one, and Angel had learned to count them too. Every day he did a great deal of running upstairs and down. Sometimes he found it hard to spend as much time with his chickens as he would like. He was sure he would miss seeing the egg hatch or miss meeting the boys coming from school, if he didn't think of some way to be able to spend more time upstairs or downstairs and not always *going* upstairs or *going* downstairs.

He thought about it when he climbed more than he did when he was running down. The steps always seemed so much longer going up than going down that he had more time to think about important problems.

He thought about it when he was at the market, sometimes so much so that he forgot to notice the beautiful smells of the spices and the fresh bread, the flowers and the leather goods.

One such day he walked through the market with his head so far down that he nearly didn't see the foreign lady who was wearing a hat. No ladies that Angel ever saw wore hats except foreign ladies. Others wore shawls over their heads, or the young ones wore flowers. But no hats!

This one wore a dress of some soft-looking cloth, and silk stockings and white shoes with brown trimming. She had a strap on her shoulder with a box hanging to it. Her hair was pretty too—sort of a red and gold color, what he could see of it. She looked very pretty, but she couldn't talk very well. Angel heard her and, although it sounded funny, he didn't laugh because that wasn't polite.

Some of the other boys crowded around her trying to get her to let them carry the things she had bought. But Angel had been brought up to be more courteous. He had also been taught not to stare, but he forgot that and watched the lady and the boys until the lady noticed him and beckoned.

When he was near enough, the lady asked his name.

"Angel, at your service, Señorita."

"And it is what I need, service! Angel, will you please carry my things?"

Angel had never done anything like that before except for his mother, but it would be rude to refuse to help a lady. So he said, "With great pleasure," although he didn't really mean it.

She loaded him with the oddest assortment of things—a pineapple and a toy stove, a bunch of bananas, some dishes, a copper pan, some embroidered cloth, and finally a big bunch of lilies. Since none of these was wrapped, he had difficulty in holding them all until he motioned the lady to a stall where they sold a long bag with a string at each end.

The lady couldn't comprehend the flow of Spanish that went with his suggestion, but she understood the idea and bought the bag at the first price asked, which was very odd.

Angel loaded the cloth, the bananas, the pineapple and the dishes into the bag and slung the strap over his right shoulder and under his left arm, so that his cargo was safe on his back. Then he put the pan on his head, carried the stove in one hand and the flowers in the other. The lady and Angel both laughed, and the lady took his picture with the camera she took out of the box on the string. All the other boys wanted to get into the picture too, but Angel told them that if the lady wanted their picture she would have asked

him to so request them. Therefore they should be polite and withdraw.

The boys contented themselves with standing behind and beside him, and did not stand in front of him. The lady took the picture, and she and Angel started off.

Everyone looked at the pretty lady, and Angel felt very proud to have been selected to carry her purchases. However, so many of the other boys followed that Angel felt compelled now and then to try to drive them away. Each time this happened the lady would keep on walking and Angel would have to run to catch up. By the time he'd caught up with her again, the boys were once more at his heels. So after a while Angel didn't try any more.

He pretended to himself that it was a religious procession and that he was part of it. He'd never been in a procession but had seen many of them. This was almost as good, he decided, and here he was up near the front. In any real processions all the boys were near the end. Maybe this was even better, now that he thought about it. He had flowers in his arms just like in the procession. Of course, he wouldn't have the toy stove, but he could pretend that that was a prayer book.

Angel was just beginning to enjoy his idea thoroughly when they arrived at the hotel where the lady lived. When he realized that he was invited in, he was delighted. He'd never been in such a place before, and his eyes darted from one thing to another as he noticed things he must remember to tell his mother about.

He carefully placed the flowers on a table, removed the pan from his head, and placed that and the stove under the table. Then he unpacked the pineapple and placed it in the pan, put the dishes on the table, the bananas on one of the plates, and folded the embroidery and the bag. The lady was getting something out of her box again. Angel decided she was going to take a picture of her purchases and arranged them carefully.

But it wasn't the camera she took out. It was her purse—and from it a peso. And she gave it to Angel.

Angel's eyes grew bigger than the plates he'd just unpacked. A whole peso! Many boys and girls worked for a month as house servants for four or five pesos. However, it would not be honest to take it. He had not earned it.

"No, thank you, señorita. It was for nothing that I did it."

"But it is not for pay. It is as a present."

That was different.

"But I have nothing to give you for a present," Angel replied. "Although it is nearing Christmas, and after that will be the Epiphany, the time for the giving of presents, I have none to give."

"But you have given me a service, which was a very fine present. So I give a present to you."

Angel considered this. Finally he decided that it would be all right.

"A thousand thanks," he said gravely. "You are my friend."

"Yes," said the lady, shaking hands with him, "we are friends."

"You will come to see me?" she asked as he went to the door.

"If you wish."

"Yes, come again tomorrow."

"Thank you," he said and closed the door quietly.

But once out on the street again, he was assailed by all the boys who had followed them from the market and who had wanted to find out what the lady had paid Angel.

"A peso! A peso!" he exclaimed again and again. One big fellow made a lunge at him.

"Let me see it," the big boy demanded, but Angel eluded him and ran all the way home so fast that his shadow had trouble keeping up with him.

His mother saw that he was excited, but she was herself too busy getting supper ready to want to listen to him, even if he had had the breath and the voice to tell the story at once.

"Please get me some water, quickly, quickly!" she said at once.

Angel was glad of the delay in telling the story, but sorry to have to go back down the stairs. "Yes, Mother," he said, and put the coin into his pocket. But though he got the water at once, it was not quickly. His legs were tired, and this time he had time to think on the way up.

He thought again about his walk with the lady. He saw himself walking down the street a little behind her. People looked out of their doorways and smiled. No wonder everyone smiled at her, he thought. She is very pretty and very kind. He thought about the bananas and the boys who had followed him. He felt again the warmth of the sunshine and the cool of the shadows as they walked through the park under the shade of one tree after another. He thought of the hotel, a beautiful new hotel. Why, it wasn't even quite finished! The masons were still working on it. Suddenly the idea came to him. The masons! He had seen them lift their bricks and mortar with a rope! That would do it! A rope was what he needed.

How wonderful to have received today a whole peso, and now to know how to save himself so many trips up and down stairs! He was so happy that he was almost able to run up the rest of the stairs in spite of being so tired.

His chickens needed to be fed and given fresh water. Here it was, time to ring his bell, and then it was time for supper. He ate hungrily, but both his father and his mother saw how excited he was. They talked of other things and waited.

Finally, "It cannot be bad," said Miguel. "Our son looks too happy."

"No, nor can he have come to any difficulty, or he would have asked our help."

"Oh, Mother! Father!" Angel almost burst saying it. "It is so wonderful."

"Yes, it must be!" they said, laughing, "to keep you quiet for so long."

Angel was groping in his pocket for his coin. Now he laid it on the table, put his hand over it, and, when he was sure that he had their attention, he drew his hand away.

"Look!"

He needn't have said it. Miguel and María looked!

"But how did you get that?" "Where did it come from?" It was only his own excitement that enabled him to get the story of the peso told between their eager questions.

"But who is this lady?" Even when the story had been told, the questions didn't stop.

"I do not know her name, Father. She stays at the hotel."

"But she may teach our boy bad things. If she lives at the hotel she must have much money. How are we to know that she has it honestly?"

"Oh no, Mama, she will not teach me bad things! She cannot teach me at all. Why, she can hardly talk!"

"She cannot talk? Oh, the poor lady!"

"Oh, she can talk, but not well. She says things funny. She twists her words around and says them so you can hardly understand."

"Ah, she has money, but no education. The poor lady!"

"Yet you can see she has a kind heart, Miguel. It is well that our boy should go to help her. He can teach her to speak correctly."

And so it was decided.

8

Each day María tried to remember at one time all the things she needed from the market for the day so that Angel would have time to go to help the foreign lady who needed him so much.

Angel had a very busy time. There was the bell to ring, the chickens to feed and clean and water, and the trip to the market. There he had to meet the boys and learn a word from them. And now he had to visit the lady to help her, but he knew it was his duty to help those less fortunate.

Each day Angel and the lady went to a different place. Once to the Placo de Charros where the beautiful horses and the men in their velvet suits with silver embroidery delighted the lady as much as they did Angel.

That day the lady bought a serape, but Angel wouldn't let her pay the first price asked, but bargained for it as if he had done so all his life.

"You are a real businessman!" the lady praised him as he picked up the serape.

"Thank you. I learned from my mother," he answered modestly, feeling very proud. "She always buys carefully."

When Angel left her, the lady gave him five pesos.

Angel was aghast! "But I can't take all that money!" he objected. "I have done nothing."

"Oh, you have! You saved me twice that much today. I am giving it to you not as pay but as a commission."

Angel thought about it. He had never heard of a commission, but if it was not pay he thought it might be all right.

"Thank you," he said. "As a commission."

The five pesos went with the one peso into María's hand for safekeeping.

Another day it was to the old fort on the hill. They carried a lunch and ate it there. Angel told the lady about the siege of the city and the hole in the dome of the cathedral. As they ate lunch, Angel tasted things he'd never eaten before because they were too expensive: cake and fruits and milk and bread and butter. They were good, but he didn't like them as much as tortillas, he decided. He wondered why the lady, if she had all that money to spend, hadn't bought tortillas.

That day the lady gave Angel two pesos. Angel said, "Oh no, I couldn't accept money for being your guest at a delicious dinner."

But the lady said, "No, it is not pay. It is my fare. If I had gone up there on the bus I should have paid fare, but you showed me the way so that I could walk. So since you brought me there, instead of the bus, you deserve the fare."

Angel saw that this was reasonable. "Thank you," he said, and took the money to his mother.

And so each day the money grew until by the end of the week there were eleven pesos. But then the lady had to leave the beautiful hotel and return to her own country. Angel went down early on the day she was leaving to say good-by to her. She was standing in the patio, and as soon as she saw him she came out quickly saying, "I hoped you'd come soon. Let us go to the market together. I want to buy a present for you, so that you will remember what a nice time we had together. What would you like me to buy you?"

Angel thought of how hard his mother worked to wash his clothes in the water that he carried up the stairs. Maybe he could help her.

"Would the Señorita think it too much to ask if I

should mention a cake of soap?" he inquired politely.

"No. You shall have the soap, but I want it to be something for yourself as well."

Angel thought of how worn his father's sandals were, and after all he was a man and could not go barefooted like a child. It was very much to ask, but would the Señorita think he was too grasping if he should ask for new straps for his father's sandals?

The lady laughed, although Angel could see no joke in what he'd said, but he smiled politely. "Would that be too much?" he hazarded.

"Of course not," she assured him. "Your father shall have the new straps. But you yourself, isn't there something you have always wanted to have? A toy maybe, or clothes, or something to eat?"

Angel didn't answer. He was too aghast at the idea. It was gigantic, but maybe he should tell her.

The lady watched him. "Tell me!" she asked. "What would you like?"

"A rope!" he gasped. "A long rope!"

"A rope?" she repeated.

"Yes, to make it easier to carry things upstairs." The whole plan tumbled from his lips—the water-carrying, the marketing, the chickens—and the lady understood, although sometimes Angel talked so fast that she had to ask him to tell parts of the plan twice or three times.

"A very good plan!" she exclaimed again and again throughout the story.

When he had finished, she got her little box. "Now let us go at once and find the right rope," she said, taking his hand in hers.

First they went back to look at the side of the hotel where the masons were working. The lady asked them to tell her the best place to buy a strong long rope. They looked at her in a strange way, but she just smiled and they smiled back and told her that there was a very good man in the corner of the market near the sandal-maker. She thanked them and asked about the pulley that was fastened to the top of the building. Was it expensive? And how did one purchase such things? If the men looked surprised before, they looked amazed now! But she smiled some more and they smiled back and told her that there were some very good second-hand ones in the junk shop near the center of the market on the other side from the flower-seller.

"Thank you very much," said the lady politely.

"Thank you," echoed Angel importantly.

"It was nothing!" said the man.

"Tourists buy the strangest things," said the other man. "I knew one once who bought a horse and carriage and had them taken home on the boat, but I never before heard of a lady who bought a pulley."

But by then Angel and the lady were too far away to hear what he said.

At the market they first bought the soap and sandal-straps and then looked for the other things. It was as the man had said. They found the pulley and bought it. Then they went to buy the rope, but this wasn't so easy. Neither of them knew how much rope Angel needed, nor did they want to tell the man what it was to be used for. Angel only knew that he needed a great deal, and the lady finally bought the longest rope the man had, but she was still not sure it was long enough. So she made a bargain with the rope-seller. She would pay him more money so that, if the rope was not long enough, Angel could have as much more rope as he needed, but if it was long enough Angel was to have half the amount back and the rope-seller might have the other half for his trouble. Moreover, the rope-seller was to help the boy get his rope home.

All the people at that corner of the market had gathered around and listened to the bargaining, so there were many witnesses to the arrangement. They all nodded their heads. "Yes, it is fair!" they decided. "Yes, we will remember!"

The man was tying the rope! Angel's eyes glowed!

"I have to catch my train now," said the lady. "Good-by, Angel. I hope your rope works well."

"Good-by, Señorita. For the present and for all

your kindness, I thank you. How shall I repay you
for all this?"

"You must name your new chicken after me," she
declared. "I have never had anyone or anything named
after me."

"It would be an honor!" Angel answered solemnly.
"And how does the Señorita call herself?"

"Fifi."

"Ah, but it is such a beautiful name for a chicken!"

"For a chicken, yes, it is fine." The lady laughed.
"Good-by, Angel."

"Not good-by, Señorita. Until another time!" corrected Angel.

"Yes, until another time," she answered.

Angel watched her as she disappeared in the crowd. Then he returned to his home carrying the pulley, following the man with the big hank of rope, and followed by all the small boys of the neighborhood. "What a very fine procession!" Angel thought, swinging the pulley as an incense burner. "I shall know just how to behave in a procession if I ever get into one."

9

The next day was the most exciting that Angel could ever remember. He and his father put up the pulley! It took a long time because they had never done a job like that before, but they went up and looked at the bells to see how they were fastened and tried to make their pulley fastenings look as much like those as they could.

They hadn't finished yet when María called them to dinner. They ate as quickly as possible because they wanted to get back to their work on the pulley. Angel gathered up the crumbs and took them to the chickens, but he was back almost at once.

"She is here!" he cried. "Fifi is here!"

"What?"

"The little chicken! Her name is Fifi! And she is here!"

It was true! The egg must have hatched that morning, for a little yellow ball followed Cow around on the roof.

"Her name should have been Calf!" declared María. "But hear what a big noise she makes!"

Indeed the three tried to sound like a whole flock. The rooster crowed at the new chicken, and the new chicken cheeped enough to please even María. "Ah, it is like music!" she sighed.

"If only you would say that once about my singing," Miguel teased her.

"But I say it of your bells! Is that not enough?" She laughed.

Angel had been watching Fifi, but at the mention of the bells he once more thought of the pulley. He took his father's hand in his and they went back to their work.

"My father," he said, "is it not wonderful?"

"All of life is wonderful, my son. But what is it that makes you think of that just now?"

"The chicken and the rope and we have such a fine pulley for it!"

Miguel laughed, but agreed. "Yes, it is indeed. And there are yet more wonders to come!"

"What, Father?"

"As if you did not know! Soon it will be Christmas. And then it will be Epiphany!"

"But that is a long way off, almost two weeks."

"It will be here before you know. It will be like our work—see, it is done already!"

Miguel and Angel looked at the pulley and pulled it once or twice. It was strong and secure. The boy dashed down the stairs after the rope which lay on a pile below. Back he came, puffing, with the load tied around his waist.

"Why is that?" Miguel grinned.

"Because it is heavy and I dropped it twice and had to go back for it," Angel explained. "This way I can't drop it."

Miguel untied his son and slipped the rope through the pulley. "Now, what shall we lower?" he asked.

Angel dashed into the house and got his water pail. His father tied it fast to the rope and it dropped slowly from sight as Miguel played out the rope.

Back Angel went down the stairs again. Yes, the pail was there, and enough rope remained to raise it up again. It worked so far! Untying the bucket, he ran to get water. He would fill it full this time for a test! It was very heavy, but he was so excited that he hardly noticed as he tied the pail to the rope again. He was careful about it because he didn't want the pail of water to spill. Slowly, hand over hand, he pulled, and

slowly the pail rose! It was wonderful! It worked!
Miguel unfastened the pail and called María to see

the lovely invention. She clasped her hands in delight. Miguel fastened the other pail onto the rope and lowered it again. Again Angel filled it with such speed that anyone watching would have thought the tower was afire. Again he tied it to the rope and again raised it. Miguel untied it with a flourish in front of María's admiring eyes. "Marvelous!" she exclaimed. "It is like living in a palace. It is like having a faucet in the house!"

Miguel's prophecy came true. Angel was so delighted with the pulley that he almost forgot Fifi except to feed her and admire her when he went up to ring the bells.

His mother was almost as happy with the new rope and pulley as Angel was. She untied the pails and put the empty ones on, and when the things were brought from the market, she lifted them out. When she forgot something from the market, Angel still had to run upstairs to find out what his mother wanted when she called, and María was sorry for this. To save him trouble, she volunteered to learn to write the words—but she couldn't remember which was which. So Angel drew a picture of a pail under the word "water," an ear of corn under the word "corn," a pepper under its name, and so on. But "flour" and "salt" puzzled him. Finally he put a pinch of each in the proper place, and María had no more trouble. She had to copy the word each time she used it, but she didn't mind.

After she had the word written, she would put it with a few coins into the bottom of the pail and lower it to the ground. Then Angel would come in from the court every little while to see if she had sent down a note. If there was a note in the pail he ran to the market and bought whatever his mother wanted, put it into the pail, and raised the pail aloft. The rope and pulley were quick and saved so much work that it was no wonder María and her son were happy.

Angel spent his new leisure time with his friends from the school, who were now on vacation. They taught him to count, and each time he climbed the stairs he counted them. There were 197 steps, he knew now. He had counted them over and over again.

Then the boys taught him to write his name and "Joyous Christmas" and "Prosperous New Year." Angel was so busy and happy that Christmas seemed to come when he had looked the other way for a moment.

Suddenly it was Christmas Eve. There had been the visits of the nine days before, when the children had pantomimed the search for lodgings of Mary and Joseph, there had been the piñata to make, and the bells to ring much oftener than usual for all the extra church services, and now tonight there was to be the biggest procession of all, and the lights! To Angel they were the most exciting part of Christmas. The lamps were all filled and waiting to be lighted under the bells. Angel had helped his father with this, running up to the top of the tower and back to his home, again and again.

But once, coming from the tower, he saw that María looked very tired. "Can I help you, Mother?"

"No, my son, it is nothing!"

Again he came in and asked his mother, "Are you not well?"

She answered, "I am all right, but ask your father to come to me if he is not busy."

Angel went for his father at once and returned with him. "It was not so important." María smiled. "Angel, run and play."

The boy knew that he was being sent away, but not why. He went out and looked at the chickens, but they were all asleep and didn't want to be disturbed. He would have gone up to see the bells, but he had just left them and knew they were all right. He stood looking over the city for a little while and then went back into the room.

His mother did not speak, but his father said quickly, "Angel, will you get me some water?"

Never before had Miguel asked him for anything. It was always María. Without answering, Angel ran

from the room and down the stairs. He untied the pail and ran across the court between the crowds of people gathering for Midnight Mass. Dressed in their best clothes, they were startled to see a little boy clutching an empty gasoline can darting among them. One or two tried to stop him to ask where he was going so fast at midnight on Christmas Eve, but he didn't wait.

Coming back with the filled pail, Angel had an even harder time getting through the traffic and the people. He was confused both by the lights of the houses and cars and by the darkness of the park. It

was like a nightmare of honking horns, calling people and legs! Everywhere, legs!

Finally he reached the rope and tied the pail. Grasping the rope, he pulled it up as fast as he could. A little water splashed from the side, so he pulled more slowly. He had to wait just a little while before his father removed it and tied on the empty pail, but it seemed a long long time. When the second pail was down, there was a larger crowd, more confusion and more trouble than the last time. It was harder to get to the fountain and harder yet to get back. People pushed him and said, "Wait, my young fellow, it is not good to be rude going to Mass!" and "We are all trying to get in too. Don't shove us so!" He had so much trouble that it seemed he'd never get back to his mother.

Tying the pail to the rope this time was harder, for his hands trembled and he was very tired. Finally it was tight, and he pulled the other end of the rope. Up went the pail, and not a moment too soon, for the Archbishop himself was coming in, leading the procession to say Mass! Angel was afraid that he would be seen, for the crowd was melting away to make room for the little old man in the church vestments, for the boys bearing candles, for the priests and deacons and subdeacons. It was a beautiful procession and they were coming right toward Angel.

Angel pulled harder and faster, but he must have jerked the rope because he was frightened. Suddenly the pail must have tipped, for a big, big splash of the cold water descended from the darkness of the top of the tower and—horror of horrors—it splashed right on top of his excellency, the Archbishop!

Angel was so terrified he didn't know what to do! He clutched the rope tighter than ever, his eyes open wide and his knees trembling so that he thought he would fall. But he couldn't say anything.

The Archbishop didn't say anything either.

However, they were the only ones who didn't! Such a clamor arose that Miguel must have heard it in the tower when he removed the pail from the rope because he was too excited to tie the other pail onto the rope. Since Angel was so frightened that he was holding the rope for support, he pulled the end through the pulley and—thump! The whole long heavy rope fell on top of them! The boy and the Archbishop were both covered with coils of rope.

"A snake!" "A great snake!" the cry arose.

"They are trying to kill the Archbishop!"

"The boy tried to drown him!"

His excellency gently disengaged himself and found his voice. He raised his hand. The hysterical ones were quiet.

"Please!" said the quiet voice. "There is no snake! It

is a rope. No one would kill me with a rope if I were not fastened to it!" His old face smiled, and some of the crowd giggled nervously.

"But you are all wet!" said those near to him.

"Yes, but the clothes can be changed!" He was watching Angel.

All the while the crowd had been shouting, Angel had been burrowing deeper into the coils of the rope.

"Bring me the boy—but gently, gently," said the Archbishop.

Two of the men in the crowd uncovered the cowering Angel and forced him over the pile of rope to stand before the old man. Angel was too frightened to say a word, but hung his head in silence.

A gentle old hand patted his head and turned it up so that the boy couldn't help looking into his face. Suddenly Angel realized that his excellency was not a big man. Miguel was both bigger and stronger than the Archbishop, but Angel knew that even Miguel would have been frightened now, even though the Archbishop smiled at him.

"For what was the water?" the old man asked.

"For my mother, your excellency."

"And what is your mother called?"

"María, your excellency."

"And your father?"

"Miguel, your excellency."

"Miguel, the bell-ringer?"

"The same, your excellency."

"And you?"

"Angel, your excellency."

"Where is Miguel?"

"With my mother, your excellency."

And so, piece by piece, the whole story came out. Long before the trembling boy had answered all the patient questions, dry clothes had been brought for his excellency. The boy who had brought them joined the crowd standing in shocked silence listening to all the details. Finally the Archbishop came to the part about the notes in the pail and how María was learning to write.

"How many words can you now write, son?"

"Sixty-three, your excellency."

"Do you want to go to school?"

Angel nodded his head, but could hardly form the words, "Yes, your excellency," for he knew that now that dream was over for him. He'd probably go to jail instead of school! He'd not only spilled water on a person and dropped a big rope on him, but on the very most reverend Archbishop himself! If he had one wish it was that he could fall through the floor, not go to school. "Yes, your excellency," he sobbed.

Miguel must now have heard that small sob through the great silence before and after it, because the crowd against the steps was forced open and Miguel came through to stand beside his small son. He saw the rope, and a glance at the wet vestments told him the story.

"Your most reverend excellency," he said respectfully, "I deeply regret that this accident has happened. Please do not punish the boy. He is a good boy. It is I who should be punished. I should have been more careful. I should have prevented it."

The Archbishop recognized Miguel. "Where have you been?" he asked. "The bells should have rung a half hour ago!"

"At home with my wife and my other son," Miguel answered.

"I did not know you had another son. Is he the same as this one?"

"No, your excellency, not yet!"

"How old is he, Miguel?"

"A half hour old, your excellency."

The crowd heard and turned from its anger to smiles of understanding. Angel's face brightened through his tears. "Really?" he asked.

"Really!" his father answered.

"And what will you call him?" asked the old man, smiling.

"We would be most honored if you would suggest a name, your excellency."

"On Christmas Eve what other name than 'Jesús'?

It is the most blessed of names. If he is as good a boy as Angel, it will be no blasphemy."

"Thank you, your excellency." Miguel knelt and kissed the Archbishop's ring. Angel did the same, but said, "Pardon me, your excellency!"

"Up, my boy!" said the old man. "You are a good boy and a smart boy, but I think you do not have enough to do!" His old eyes twinkled, but Angel was too frightened to notice.

"I shall be glad to do anything I can for you, your excellency! I can carry water and clean and sweep steps—"

"Stop! Stop! Enough! Enough!" The Archbishop stopped the flood of suggestions. "You must do penance for drowning me. About ten years—no, maybe more!"

Angel's tears flowed again, and his lower lip trembled. He looked up at Miguel's uncomprehending face. Ten years in prison! He would not see Jesús nor Fifi nor María nor Miguel! He hardly heard the gentle old voice continue "—in school." "IN SCHOOL!" it repeated.

"IN SCHOOL?" he shouted.

"Yes, as punishment!"

"Oh, your excellency, it would not be honest of me to let you think that would be a punishment. It would be my dearest wish."

The old Archbishop patted the boy's head. "Yes, so I thought! You have done no wrong, my boy. Don't be so frightened! I hope you will be happy there, and a blessed Christmas to you and María and Miguel and Jesús."

His clothes were dry enough now so that he might not have needed to change them, but to please the boy who had gone to the trouble of getting the dry garments, he went to put them on.

The crowd dissolved from around Miguel and Angel, and Angel suddenly felt very tired. Miguel gathered the rope in his arms, then took the boy by the hand, and together they climbed the stairs to the bells.

Angel could hardly pull his rope he was so tired, but Miguel cheered him with calls of encouragement in time to the strokes of the big bells. Just when Angel thought he couldn't pull once more, it was over, and the time for lighting the lamps was begun.

First they lighted all of them, dozens and dozens all over the floor of the tower. But then Miguel had to place them along the ledge outside. He put lighted lamps on all the ledges, in all the niches, until the whole tower was outlined in lights against the night sky. Each of these lamps in turn Angel handed to his father. His fear that his father would fall or drop a lamp was so strong that he forgot how tired he was until it was over at last. He hadn't thought he'd look forward to the lighting of the lamps being over—not when he'd looked forward to it all year—but he was glad when it was finished.

Miguel stepped in safely and took him by the hand once more. "Now let us see Jesús," he said.

María was lying with the new baby in the curve of her arm. They were both asleep, but the baby's face was turned enough so that Angel could see a little of it in the moonlight.

"He is very pretty," he said. "No, he is very handsome," he amended.

"Do you like him as much as Fifi?" his father teased.

"Yes. Of course I know Fifi better," he added defensively.

"But you like him?"

"Very much."

"Good. You are my very good big boy. You must help me to make him as good a boy as you!"

"It will be a pleasure, my father."

Quietly, in the dark, they went to the other side of the room to sleep. They had two to take care of and must not disturb them. Angel sleepily made plans. Jesús must learn not to pay the first price he is asked in the market. And he must learn how to walk so that he will look right in a procession. . . .